Contents

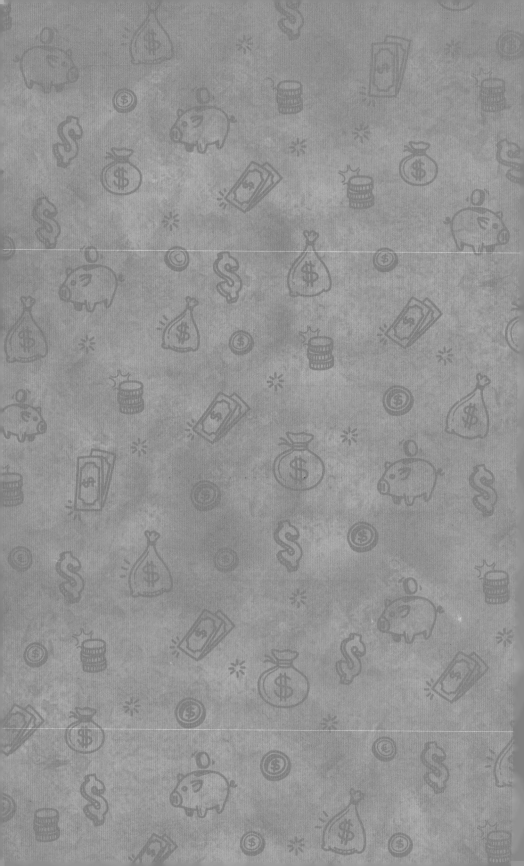

Chapter 1
Pedro's birthday

It was Pedro's birthday.

His grandma gave him a funny

card. It had lots of money in it!

"Wow!" yelled Pedro. "Thank

you, Grandma. I am rich!"

"I have lots of money too,"
said Katie. "I keep it in a
piggy bank. I love shaking my
money and making it jingle."

"I keep my money in a glass jar," said JoJo. "I can see it when I shake it!"

JoJo asked Pedro, "Where
do you keep your money?"

"I keep mine in a box,"
said Pedro. "I love to count it."

"You can put some money

in the bank," said Pedro's dad.

"It will be safe, and your money

will grow."

"Wow!" said Pedro. "I hope

my money grows as tall as you!"

Chapter 2
Future plans

Pedro and his dad went to

the bank. Pedro gave them a

lot of his money, but he kept

some of it.

Later, Pedro told Katie and JoJo, "My money is growing in the bank. Maybe it will grow as high as a mountain!"

"My money is growing too," said Katie. "I will buy my dad a gold watch. He will never be late again."

"I'm getting my mum a new car," said JoJo. "The car will be shiny red, like her lipstick."

"Cool!" said Pedro. "We can all go for a ride."

Pedro told Katie and JoJo,
"I have a bit of money to
spend today. What should
I do with it?"

"You should get an ice cream," said Katie. "Ice cream is a good way to spend money."

"It really is!" said Pedro.

"I will do that."

Chapter 3
Time for a treat

On the way to the shop,

the three friends saw Roddy.

"Let's play football," said Roddy.

"That's a good idea!" said
Pedro. "I can get an ice cream
later."

Pedro kicked the ball hard.

He kicked and ran. 2③ di/gir

Whoops!

His money went flying out

of his pocket. The wind blew it

away!

"I'll help you find it," said Katie.

"Us too," said JoJo and Roddy.

They looked in the tall grass and the trees. They found all the money!

"Thank you," said Pedro. "This is a lot of money. I can buy myself ice cream cones all week!"

"That's right," said Katie.

"You can have a new

flavour every day," said JoJo.

"Lucky you," said Roddy.

They began walking away.

"Wait!" yelled Pedro.

"I know the best way to eat ice cream."

"How?" asked his friends.

"With you," said Pedro. "The ice cream is my treat for all of you!"

"Yay!" yelled everyone.

They each had a different
flavour. All of the cones tasted
cool and sweet.

"Feeling happy is as much
fun as feeling rich," said
Pedro.

And it was!

About the author

Fran Manushkin is the author of Katie Woo, the highly acclaimed early-reader series, as well as the popular Pedro series. Her other books include *Happy in Our Skin*, *Baby, Come Out!* and the bestselling board books *Big Girl Panties* and *Big Boy Underpants*. There is a real Katie Woo: Fran's great-niece, but she doesn't get into as much trouble as the Katie in the books. Fran lives in New York City, USA, three blocks from Central Park, where she can often be found birdwatching and daydreaming. She writes at her dining room table, without the help of her naughty cats, Goldy and Chaim.

About the illustrator

Tammie Lyon's love of drawing began at a young age while sitting at the kitchen table with her dad. She continued to pursue art and eventually attended the Columbus College of Art and Design in Ohio, USA, where she earned a bachelor's degree in fine art. After a brief career as a professional ballet dancer, she decided to devote herself full time to illustration. Today she lives with her husband, Lee, in Ohio. Her dogs, Gus and Dudley, keep her company as she works in her studio.

Glossary

bank a business that stores and lends money

flavour the kind of taste in a food

jingle to make a light clinking sound

money the coins and notes that people use to buy things

shiny very polished and bright

Let's talk

1. What sort of container do each of the main characters keep their money in? Which one would you choose for your money?

2. How do you think Pedro felt when he lost his money? Have you ever lost something? How did you feel?

3. At the end of the story, Pedro says, "Feeling happy is as much fun as feeling rich". Do you agree with him?

Let's write

1. Pedro and his friends talk about what they want to buy others. If you could buy something big for someone special in your life, what would you buy? Who would you give it to?

2. Design your own piggy bank by drawing a picture. Write a sentence to describe it.

3. Pretend you are Pedro and write your grandma a thank-you note for your birthday money. Make sure you say what you did with the money.

Where does a penguin keep its money?
In a snow bank

What did the pound coin name its daughter?
Penny

What is brown and has a head and a tail but no legs?
A penny

When does it rain money?
When there's a change in the weather

How did the dinosaur pay at the restaurant?
With Tyrannosaurus cheques!

Where did the frog put its money?
In the river bank

Why did Pedro put his money in the freezer?
He wanted cold, hard cash.

HAVE MORE FUN WITH PEDRO!

   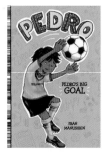